Kidnapped

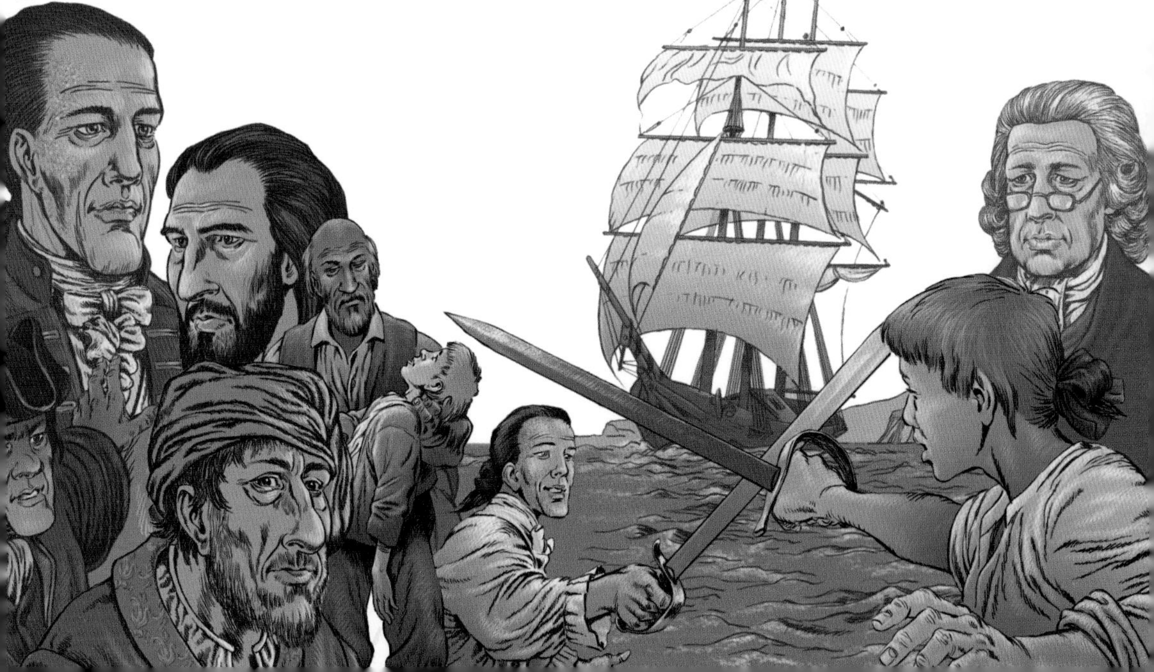

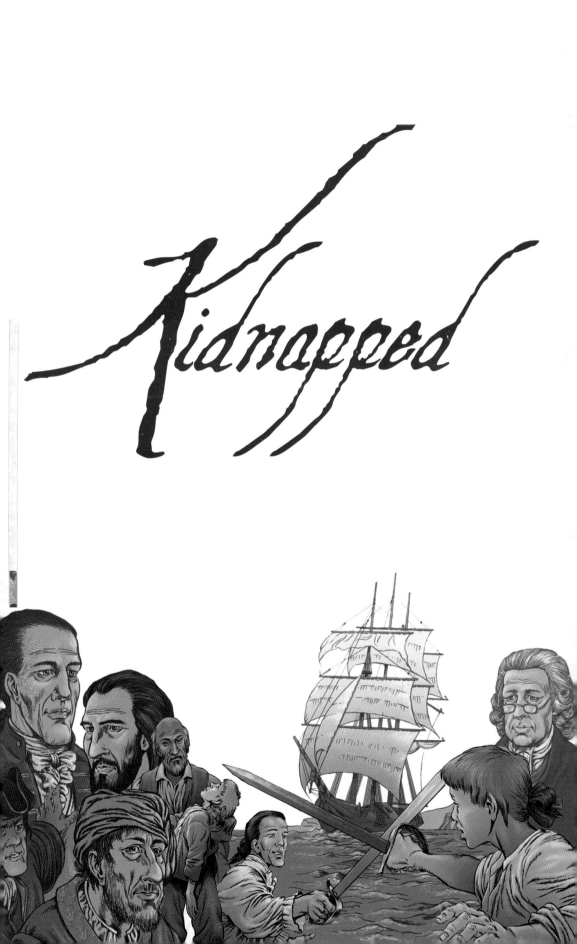

Acknowledgments

Artists: Penko Gelev
Sotir Gelev

First edition for North America (including Canada and Mexico), Philippine Islands,
and Puerto Rico published in 2007 by Barron's Educational Series, Inc.

All inquiries should be addressed to:
Barron's Educational Series, Inc.
250 Wireless Boulevard
Hauppauge, NY 11788
www.barronseduc.com

ISBN-13 (Hardcover): 978-0-7641-5980-0
ISBN-10 (Hardcover): 0-7641-5980-1
ISBN-13 (Paperback): 978-0-7641-3494-4
ISBN-10 (Paperback): 0-7641-3494-9

Library of Congress Control No.: 2005936255

Photo credits:
p41 ©Thomas Herter, http://pbase.com/goislands
p44 Sportsphoto
p45 ©The Salariya Book Company Ltd. 2007
p47 (top) TopFoto/HIP TopFoto.co.uk (bottom) Steve Trussel

Every effort has been made to trace copyright holders. The Salariya Book Company apologizes
for any omissions and would be pleased, in such cases, to add an acknowledgment in future editions.

Printed and bound in China
9 8 7 6 5 4 3 2 1

Kidnapped

Robert Louis Stevenson

Illustrated by
Penko Gelev

BARRON'S

Retold by
Fiona Macdonald

Series created and designed by
David Salariya

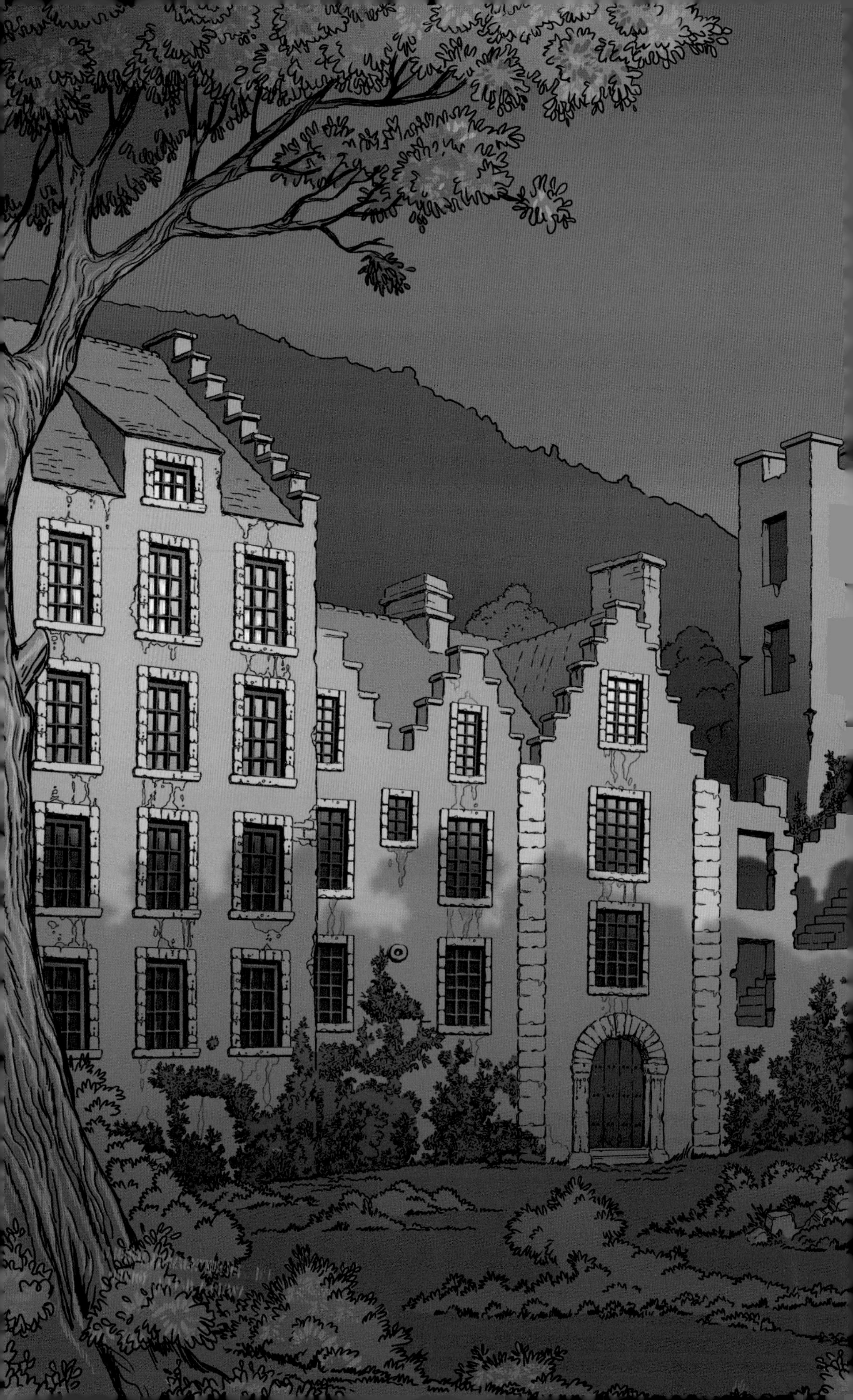

The nearer I got to that, the drearier it appeared. It seemed like the one wing of a house that had never been finished. What should have been the inner end stood open on the upper floors, and showed against the sky with steps and stairs of uncompleted masonry. Many of the windows were unglazed, and bats flew in and out like doves out of a dove-cote.

CHARACTERS

David Balfour

Ebenezer Balfour

Mr. Rankeillor, lawyer

Captain Hoseason,
owner of the *Covenant*

Mr. Riach,
ship's doctor

Mr. Shuan,
ship's mate

Ransome,
cabin boy

Alan Breck, Jacobite rebel

Colin Campbell of Glenure,
nicknamed the "Red Fox"

James Stewart, nicknamed
"James of the Glens"

Cluny Macpherson,
Highland clan chief

Robin Oig Macgregor,
outlaw

The "Bonnie Lass"

Scotland, 1751

I will go with you as far as the ford[1] to set you on your way.

David Balfour walks past the churchyard where both his parents lie buried. Just 18 years old, he must leave his village of Essendean* to find a new home, a new job, and a new family.

Old Mr. Campbell, the Minister,[2] has come to say goodbye. He hands over a letter written by David's father shortly before he died.

David reads: "To Ebenezer Balfour Esquire[3]. . . in his house of Shaws . . . will be delivered by my son David." Who is Ebenezer? Where is Shaws? David wants to know more.

Gifties.[4]

The Minister says that Shaws* is a grand house at Cramond, near Edinburgh. And, since Ebenezer has David's surname, perhaps they belong to the same family?

David starts to open the "gifties" that the Minister has given him. Then he watches, near to tears, as the old man walks away.

David is young, strong, and bright, but he has never traveled far. The Minister's "gifties" are money, a Bible, and herbal medicine. Will they be enough to help him survive?

David hopes so! He starts to feel more cheerful as he sets off on his long walk to find Cramond, Ebenezer, and Shaws. His whole life lies ahead of him—uncertain, but exciting!

After walking for two days, David reaches Cramond. From there he can see Edinburgh—Scotland's splendid capital city. He also catches sight of the sea, for the very first time in his life!

* See map on page 42
1. ford: river crossing
2. Minister: Christian church leader
3. Esquire: title of rank, a gentleman
4. gifties: little presents

THE HOUSE OF SHAWS

> If ye'll take word from me, ye'll keep clear of the Shaws.

> Blood shall bring it down! Black be its fall!

In Cramond, David asks how he can find the house of Shaws. But people shake their heads, and won't tell him.

At last, an old woman who looks like a witch leads David to a hilltop. She points to a bleak, crumbling mansion in the valley below—then spits and curses!

David shudders in horror, then sits on a wall to think. Should he walk on to the cursed house of Shaws? Or should he turn back to Essendean? Bravely, he goes on.

> It's loaded!

It is getting dark by the time David reaches the main gate. He enters and knocks on the door.

For a long while, no one answers. David shouts as loud as he can. At last, an old man wearing nightclothes appears, holding a gun!

> Who are ye?

> They call me David Balfour.

> I'm your born uncle, Davie.

David asks to see Ebenezer, but the old man tells him to go away. David refuses—he has an important letter to deliver. Grudgingly, the old man lets him in. David walks into a huge, bare room. The only light comes from a miserable fire.

The old man snatches the letter. David protests, but the old man insists that it is meant for him. He is Ebenezer Balfour!

Your mother... she was a bonnie lassie![1]

Well, sir... I'll stay a while.

Ebenezer gives David cold porridge for supper, and leads him to a damp, dark room. Then he locks the door. David is a prisoner!

Next morning, Ebenezer explains that he is David's father's brother. He talks about David's parents and the rich, proud Balfour family.

Ebenezer promises to share the Balfours' money with David, but David does not trust him. Scared, he threatens to leave Shaws; Ebenezer begs him to stay.

It says "To my brother Ebenezer on his fifth birthday."

What gars[3] ye ask that?

Ebenezer lets David explore a room full of dusty old books. One has David's father's neat, stylish writing in it.

David asks whether his father was older than Ebenezer. In reply, Ebenezer flies into a rage. David is mystified.[2]

With a great effort, Ebenezer controls his temper. He pretends to be sorry and gives David a gift: 37 guineas![4]

And see here... tit for tat.[5]

My uncle is trying to kill me!

In return for the money, Ebenezer asks David to fetch a locked chest from the tower. It is a wild and stormy night.

In total darkness, David stumbles up the stairs. Then a sudden flash of lightning stops him just in time—the stairs end in mid-air without any warning.

1. bonnie lassie: pretty girl
2. The grown-up handwriting makes David think that his father must have been older than Ebenezer. But if David's father was the eldest son, he—not Ebenezer—should have inherited the house. Why didn't he?
3. gars: makes
4. guineas: very valuable gold coins, worth 21 shillings (one pound and one shilling) each
5. tit for tat: one good turn deserves another

KIDNAPPED!

Ah!

Bleeaargh!

Shocked and angry, David creeps down the stairs and back into the house of Shaws. He grabs Ebenezer.

The blue phial[2]...

Ebenezer collapses. While he is unconscious, David hunts for a weapon to protect himself and finds a rusty dirk.[1] He helps Ebenezer sit up; then, he gives him medicine.

It's my heart!

Ebenezer gasps and groans. David doesn't feel sorry for him—he is too angry. He asks a lot of questions, but Ebenezer is too weak to answer. David locks him up.

Well, sir, what cause have you to attempt[3] my life?

The next morning, David unlocks Ebenezer's door. Now he intends to find out why his uncle wants to murder him.

What cheer, mate?

Ebenezer says that it was only a joke, but David does not believe him. He is about to say so when there is a loud knock at the door.

I have a venture with this man Hoseason.

The caller is a cabin boy[4] with a message for Ebenezer. It is from Captain Hoseason, master of the cargo ship *Covenant*.

Ebenezer says they must go to see Hoseason at the port of Queensferry.* As they walk, Ransome, the cabin boy, chatters to David.

I have never felt such pity for anyone.

Ransome is a strange, silly and simple-minded boy. He describes life on board ship and tells how the crewmen bully and beat him all the time.

At last they reach Queensferry, where the River Forth flows into the sea. Ransome points out the *Covenant* anchored offshore.

* See map on page 42
1. dirk: dagger
2. phial: small bottle
3. attempt: threaten
4. cabin boy: boy working as a servant on a ship

Ebenezer leads them to an inn, where Captain Hoseason is waiting. It is terribly hot indoors, so David goes outside.

David walks to the water's edge. The smell of the sea is strange and exciting. He is fascinated by seaweed, which he's never seen before.

David goes back to the inn. The landlord stares at him and then says he looks just like Ebenezer's dead brother, Alexander.

He tells David that Alexander owned Shaws but Ebenezer took it from him. Now that Alexander is dead, Shaws should belong to his son.

Hoseason comes to find David and invites him to look around his ship while it is at still at anchor.

Ebenezer encourages David to go. They all walk down to the quayside. The ship looks so interesting that David happily agrees to go onboard.

Sailors row David, Ebenezer, and Hoseason out to the *Covenant*. Hoseason climbs up the side, and David is winched aboard.

As David stands on deck, he sees the sailors start to row Ebenezer back to the shore. He is trapped on board! He has been kidnapped!

DEATH ON BOARD

David struggles and tries to leap into the sea. But he's knocked senseless by one of the sailors.

When David wakes up, his wrists are bound, he's wet and cold, and he can't see anything. His head hurts, and he feels seasick.

He faints and falls into a deep, uneasy sleep. Meanwhile, the ship sails on, far out to sea. Hours later, David wakes and hears footsteps approaching.

It's Riach, the ship's doctor. He bandages David's wounded head and helps him sip some brandy and water.

David lies for days in the ship's filthy, stinking hold.[1] Rats scurry over him, and he develops a fever.

Riach brings Captain Hoseason down to the hold and tells him that David needs fresh air and sunlight.

If David stays tied up in the hold, he will surely die, and Captain Hoseason will have caused his death.

Riach cuts the rope from David's wrists. He is free, but too weak to stand. A sailor carries him up on deck, to the crew's quarters in the forecastle.[3]

The crew give David food and drink and make him a bed to rest on. His wounds heal, and his mind clears; slowly he grows stronger.

1. hold: cargo compartment deep inside the hull of the ship
2. flit: move
3. forecastle: cabin for ordinary seamen at the front of the ship

You and Ransome are to change berths.[1]

Run away aft[3] with ye!

David hears that the *Covenant* is a slave-ship, bound for America. He also talks to Ransome, who is still being bullied.

One night, there's a sudden commotion[2] on board; the crew look grim and frightened. Hoseason comes to find David, with an order.

David is to start doing Ransome's work. He must serve the ship's officers with food and drink and run errands for them.

As Hoseason speaks, a sailor walks in, carrying a limp, lifeless body. It is Ransome.

Ransome was killed by Shuan, the ship's mate,[4] in a drunken fury. Riach takes the bottle away from Shuan and throws it overboard.

Sit down! Ye sot[5] and swine![6]

The boy went overboard… that's what the story is.

Shuan leaps to his feet to attack Riach, but Hoseason stops him. Shuan shuffles away, slumps on his bunk, and starts to cry with self-pity.

Captain Hoseason declares that no one outside the ship must ever hear of Ransome's murder. He and Riach sit talking for hours; David brings them brandy.

1. berth: bed on board ship
2. commotion: noisy disturbance
3. aft: to the back of the ship
4. mate: second-in-command
5. sot: drunkard
6. swine: pig

ALAN BRECK

Hoseason steers his ship west. But the wind and waves are against him. The *Covenant* is blown close to the wild north coast of Scotland.

Will it run aground? Or be smashed on the rocks? Or capsize[1] in a storm? Hoseason decides to sail south and seek calmer waters.

She's struck!

The crew keeps watch, day and night, as thick fog surrounds them. Then suddenly, there's a terrible crunch.

They've smashed into a smaller boat! It splits in two and sinks, as the crew watch helplessly.

All its sailors are drowned, except for one, who is thrown toward the *Covenant*. He grabs hold of the hull and clambers aboard.

Where ye come from— we might talk of that.

The man stands exhausted and gasping on deck. He speaks like a Scotsman, but his clothes are French. Hoseason questions him suspiciously.

He says that his name is Alan Breck Stewart. He claims that he is Scottish and on the run from English soldiers.

Just a few years ago Alan Breck fought against the English in the Jacobite rebellion.[1] He wanted Scotland's Bonnie Prince Charlie[2] to be king, not England's George I.

So, in 1745, he joined Bonnie Prince Charlie's army and fought King George. But Breck's side was defeated, so he fled to France. He now needs to return there.

Breck asks Hoseason to sail to France, but the captain refuses. He won't help a Jacobite escape—that would be treason.

Half of it and I'm your man!

To persuade him, Breck opens the money-belt he's wearing. He offers Hoseason 60 guineas[3] to land him safely in Scotland. Hoseason asks for more.

He scowls when Breck says he can't offer more because the money belongs to his clan[4] chieftain.

Here's my hand upon it.

And here's mine.

Finally, Hoseason agrees to take Breck to Loch Linnhe.* Alan's clansmen, the Stewarts, live nearby and will help him.

Hoseason hurries off to talk to Riach and the crewmen. He sends David away to fetch food...

...but David hears what Hoseason says. He and Riach are plotting to kill Alan Breck and steal the money he is carrying!

* See map on page 42
1. Jacobite rebellion: a rebellion against King George I (see page 43 for more information)
2. Bonnie Prince Charlie: Charles Edward Stewart, Scottish prince, a rival to King George I
3. guineas: gold coins worth 21 shillings each—a huge amount of money at this time
4. clan: large family group all descended from the same ancestor

15

A BONNIE FIGHTER

Do you ken[1] where the pistols are?

The plotters need weapons to kill Alan Breck. But guns and swords are stored in the roundhouse,[2] where Alan is sitting. They ask David to fetch some.

They're all murderers here!

David is angry—and frightened. At first, he wants to hide. But bravely, he decides to warn Alan.

But they haven't got me yet!

Alan asks David to help him fight and gives him pistols and a cutlass[3] from the roundhouse stores. They stand on guard together.

They don't have long to wait. Riach, Hoseason, and 13 crewmen attack the roundhouse from all sides. It's a savage, bloody battle...

BANG!

Am I no a bonnie fighter?[4]

This is the song of the sword of Alan...

...but Alan and David survive! Alan sings a victory song, while David counts the bodies. Shuan and five sailors lie dying; another four are badly wounded.

1. ken: know
2. roundhouse: cabin with curved walls at the back of the ship
3. cutlass: wide, curved sword
4. Am I no a bonnie fighter?: Aren't I a good fighter?

There are not enough sailors left alive to man the *Covenant* safely. It drifts close to dangerous rocks around the Isle of Skye.*

Alan and David take turns to keep watch all night. At breakfast time, Alan praises David for his boldness and bravery.

He gives David a fine silver button, cut from his coat, as a token of his friendship.

Wherever ye go and show that button, the friends of Alan Breck will come around[1] you.

There's none of the rest of us acquaint[2] with this coast.

Captain Hoseason arrives, to say he can't steer the boat to Loch Linnhe. Now that Shuan, his best sailor, is dead, it will be too dangerous.

Set me in my own country.

But Breck won't change his plans. He must be put ashore near his clan lands.

Be it as ye will.

Hoseason is furious, but has to agree. They sail ahead through rough seas past wild, rocky shores.

I'll offer you a change.[3]

The roundhouse floor is still running with blood after the fight. Breck strikes a bargain.

He gives Hoseason brandy from the roundhouse stores, in return for buckets of clean water.

* See map on page 42
1. come around: protect
2. acquaint: familiar with or knowledgeable about
3. change: exchange

THE RED FOX

For a while, the weather is calm and fair. Hoseason steers his ship grimly. He heads for the Isle of Mull,* then the entrance to Loch Linnhe.

David tells Alan how he was kidnapped; Alan talks about the Scottish Highlands. He explains that Highland life is very different from David's life at Essendean.

Highlanders all speak Gaelic, an ancient Scottish language. Some, like Alan, can speak English too.

Highlanders are loyal to their clan chiefs, who are landowners and war-leaders. In 1745–1746, many chiefs joined the Jacobites. Now they are exiled[1] in France.

The mountains and moors of the Scottish Highlands are wild and rugged. Most Highlanders are farmers. They are poor, but they still give money to their clan chiefs—even those who were Jacobite rebels.

Every year, Alan travels secretly back from France to collect money from his chief's followers. It is a risky mission.

I call it noble.

David is impressed by the loyal Highlanders—and by Alan's bravery.

The cursed race of Campbell!

Bitterly, Alan says that one clan does not behave as nobly as the others.

 * See map on page 42
1. exiled: forced to live abroad

And who is the Red Fox?

For centuries, the Campbells and Alan's Stewart clan have been sworn enemies. Now the Red Fox is trying to destroy the Stewarts forever.

Alan can hardly speak. David has never seen anyone look so angry! With effort, Alan calms down and tells David more.

He says that Red Fox's real name is Colin Campbell of Glenure. Since 1745, he has helped the English kings fight the Jacobites.

Red Fox has hunted down Jacobite rebels, burned their houses, and taken over their farms. He turns whole families out into the cold to die!

There grows not enough heather[2] in Scotland to hide him from my vengeance![3]

Now Red Fox is attacking Highlanders who help the exiled Jacobite chieftains. He is trying to drive them out of Scotland for good.

He has soldiers to guard him, and new English laws to help him "pacify"[1] the Highlands. But Alan vows to find him and kill him, as soon as he gets the chance.

1. pacify: calm and control
2. heather: a tough, bushy plant with purple flowers, which is also a symbol of Scotland
3. vengeance: revenge

19

SHIPWRECKED!

By now, it is dusk. The wind is roaring and the waves rise high. Worried, Hoseason hurries to the roundhouse.

They are now very close to the wild south coast of Mull, with no maps or charts to guide them. Hoseason wishes that Shuan could rise from the dead and steer.

The waves crash and smash on hidden undersea reefs, while the ship rolls uncontrollably. It speeds through the sea at a great rate, driven by the wind and tide.

Alan realizes that they've reached the Torran Rocks,* famous for shipwrecks. In the moonlight, he looks white with fear.

Alan tells Hoseason to head for the shore, where the water looks calmer. But Hoseason does not trust him. He sends Riach up to the foretop[2] to keep lookout.

By now the sea is so wild that the sailors can't keep hold of the tiller.[3] Caught by the tide, the *Covenant* spins around and is smashed on the rocks.

The crew try to launch a lifeboat, but are swamped by a giant wave. David is swept overboard.

* See map on page 42
1. pilot: steer the ship through a specific route
2. foretop: lookout post near the top of the foremast (front mast)
3. tiller: the lever that controls the rudder

David clings to a piece of the broken mast. He tries to swim and is finally washed ashore, totally exhausted.

David shivers with cold, fear, and tiredness. To keep warm, he walks up and down the beach—but he doesn't find any survivors.

He's alone on a barren[1] rock, with no food, water, or company. He grows more and more miserable.

He eats shellfish, but they make him sick. Worse still, he can see several houses and farms on another, larger island. But it is too far to swim!

By the third day, David is feeling very ill. Then he sees a boat with fishermen. They wave, but sail straight past. David weeps in despair.

David believes he will die alone on the rock. He kneels and says his prayers. But then the fishermen sail by again, waving and pointing.

At last David understands what they mean—he can leave this rock at low tide. He just has to wade through shallow water, then he'll reach the Island of Mull.

1. barren: lifeless

RUN FOR YOUR LIFE

On Mull, David asks for news of the shipwreck. Were there any survivors? He learns that Alan Breck has been seen.

He hurries off to find Alan. Most of the islanders are friendly and kind: they give David food and shelter. But then he's robbed and attacked by a beggar.

I am seeking somebody.

At last David reaches Torosay,* where a ferry sails to the mainland. He tries to talk to the captain, a member of Alan Breck's clan.

The captain will not speak to him, until he sees the silver button. Then he tells David how to get to Alan's home in Appin.*

... a bold, desperate customer.

As David walks, he meets a traveling preacher. They talk of the fighting in the Highlands. The preacher warns David about Alan Breck.

A fisherman rows David across Loch Linnhe. Now he is in Appin! He sees English soldiers marching along. But how will he find Alan?

The soldiers' weapons glint brightly in the sunshine, and their red coats make quite a sight. But David feels nervous.

He hears the sound of horsemen approaching, so he leaves the road and waits under some trees by the roadside.

Along with servants and a lawyer is Colin Campbell—Red Fox himself, Alan Breck's great enemy! David steps into view.

22   * See map on page 42

I am dead!
Oh I am dead!

The murderer!
Here! I see him!

Jouk[1] in here!

As he speaks to them, there's a sudden shot. Red Fox staggers. For a moment, David is too surprised to move.

Then he comes to his senses. He turns to chase a man who's disappearing into the bushes. As David runs, the soldiers aim and fire at him.

They think he is helping the murderer! From behind a tree David hears a voice.

It's Alan Breck! What luck! Together, they run as fast as they can, away from Red Fox and the soldiers' guns.

They leap over rocks, bogs, and streams, and crawl through bracken and heather. David is exhausted, but he has to keep on moving.

Do as I do, for your life!

I swear!

After a quarter of an hour, they stop to rest. Now they're out of sight of the soldiers.

It's time, Alan says, to turn around and creep back, behind the troops who are chasing them.

They reach the woods and collapse. As they recover, David asks Alan why he shot and killed Red Fox. Angrily, Alan denies it.

1. jouk: duck; crouch down and hide

JAMES OF THE GLENS

Night falls and the soldiers call off their search until the morning. David and Alan leave the woods and start walking.

They climb a hill and look down. They see lights at Aucharn,* home of Alan's kinsman,[1] James Stewart of the Glens. Alan whistles a signal.

It's Appin that must pay.

James greets them warmly, but he's terribly worried. He fears the Campbells will attack the Stewarts, now that Red Fox—a Campbell— is dead.

James's servants and children are busy hiding weapons—since 1746, it has been a crime to have them in the house.

Troth, no![2]

If the Campbells find Alan's French clothes, the Stewarts will be hanged as traitors. Should they bury the clothes?

James Stewart's wife sits by the fire, weeping uncontrollably. If the Campbells attack, what will happen to her husband and her children?

I am poor company.

James tries to talk calmly to David and Alan, but he can't sit still and paces up and down.

James's sons bring David Highland brogues[3] and clean clothes to replace the tattered, salt-stained ones he is wearing.

Ye must find a safe bit[4] somewhere nearby.

James gives Alan and David provisions for their journey: oatmeal to eat, brandy as medicine, pistols, a sword, and some money. He tells them to hide.

* See map on page 42
1. kinsman: close relative
2. troth, no!: certainly not!
3. brogues: Highland shoes with laces
4. bit: little place

24

It would be an ill day for Appin.

James says that he must pretend to help Red Fox's soldiers hunt for Alan and David. If the soldiers suspect that James has helped them, they will kill him.

Alan says that James's death would be a dreadful thing for the whole Stewart clan.

James then tells him that there's something more he must do, to protect the Stewarts from Campbell suspicion.

He must put up public notices describing Alan and David and offering a reward for their capture. Alan protests: this isn't fair. The murder of Red Fox has nothing to do with them!

David asks why the posters don't name the man who really killed Red Fox. James and Alan are horrified. They think the murderer is a Stewart, and they could never betray a clansman.

Bless God!

Bravely, David says he doesn't mind being accused if it helps Alan, James, and the Stewarts. Though secretly afraid, he really wants to be loyal to these good friends.

Hearing this, James's wife leaps up and hugs him. Again and again, she thanks him dearly for his kindness to her family.

It's near dawn, and time for David and Alan to go. The hunt for them will start again at sunrise. Red Fox's soldiers will search the whole of Appin, to catch them and kill them!

TRAPPED IN GLENCOE

Alan and David hurry over rough, rocky ground. But in the dark, they take a wrong turn. They find themselves at the bottom of a steep, narrow valley.

It's as good as a trap! They can easily be seen from the mountains all around. They must hide, right away.

Alan spies a huge boulder on the far side of the valley, but they must cross a fast, rushing river to reach it. He jumps...

...and lands on a slippery rock in the middle of roaring water. Now it's David's turn. Can he make it?

Yes! But he is shaking like a leaf and doubts he'll reach the far side. He makes a desperate leap toward dry land...

...but falls into the water! Alan grabs him and hauls him onto the bank. Now, right away, they must start running.

They reach the boulder, but they're not safe yet. They must climb right up on top of it, where Alan thinks he sees a hollow.

But the rock is smooth. How can they climb up? After three tries, Alan succeeds. He helps David scramble up after him—then peers all around the valley.

Alan sighs with relief. No one can see them here. But they're still in terrible danger. They're on the run, in wild, dangerous country, and their enemies are approaching.

David sleeps while Alan keeps watch as Red Fox's soldiers get closer. For a terrible moment when David snores, Alan thinks the soldiers will hear him.

I tell you, it's 'ot!

The sun is merciless and the rock has no shade or water. By mid-afternoon, they are burned, blistered, and desperately thirsty.

They have to move. Can they take the risk? Unseen by the soldiers, they slide down and hide among the heather.

Slowly, painfully, choking in the dust, they creep toward the river. Every twig they snap seems to echo out loud. But the English soldiers don't hear them.

Water! They drink their fill, then hide until sunset. David longs to sleep, but he knows that night is the only safe time for them to travel.

Alan whistles quietly to himself as they stumble through the darkness. Tomorrow they may die, but, amazingly, he is still cheerful!

SAFE HIDEAWAY

At dawn the next day, Alan and David finally reach a safe hiding place. It is a cave high in the mountains, close to the sea—and very well hidden!

Here they can rest and build up their strength for the next part of their journey. They swim, catch fish, and laze beside the stream.

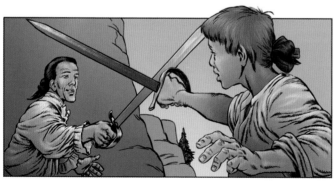

Alan tries to teach David how to fight with a long, heavy broadsword. David does his best, but Alan is impatient and often loses his temper.

How?

We must get word sent to James. He will find the siller.[1]

All the time, they discuss plans for getting to France. They can't stay in the cave forever! But to travel, they need money.

1. siller: money (silver coins)

Alan makes a wooden cross—a Stewart clan sign—and ties a silver button to it. He adds twigs from pine and birch trees that grow close to the cave.

After dark, he creeps down to the nearest village. He leaves the cross outside the house of a fellow-clansman, John Breck MacColl.

MacColl cannot read or write, but he understands Alan's sign. The next day he calls to see them at the cave.

Alan asks him to carry a secret message to James of the Glens. MacColl is very frightened, but loyally agrees.

Three days later, MacColl returns. He brings a letter—and news of fresh danger! There are hundreds of soldiers hunting for Alan…

…and James is in prison! Soldiers have arrested him for helping Red Fox's murderer.

The letter is from James's wife. She sends money and a copy of the poster offering a reward for the capture of David and Alan.

Na, troth! A fine sight I would be.

The poster lists Alan's French clothes, which make him easily recognized. But Alan bravely declares that he won't change them.

With great relief, David sees that the description of him is wrong. With luck, no one will recognize him. By himself, he'd be safe—but how could he possibly desert Alan?

CLUNY'S CAGE

It's time to go! They leave the cave and head east through wild, lonely mountains. They reach the edge of grim, ghostly Rannoch Moor,* the most desolate place in Scotland.

Somehow, they have to get across this vast, windswept, treacherous bog. They drop to the ground and crawl. Slowly they slither over the treacherous, slimy surface.

The mud seeps into their eyes and mouths, and sticks horribly to their hair. It smells sour, rotten, sickly.

But they can't stand up. They'd sink into the bog and suffocate—or be spotted by the soldiers scanning the moor's bleak, treeless skyline.

Exhausted, Alan and David rest. But soon they have to leap up and run for their lives—the soldiers are getting closer!

They are hot, tired, hungry, thirsty, bitten, scratched, and bleeding. David can't go on.

They stumble to the edge of the Moor—and are surrounded! Four wild Highlanders grab them and march them off to a most extraordinary building...

30   * See map on page 42

Step in by,[1] the both of ye.

Made of moss and branches, "Cluny's Cage" is the hideout of clan chief Cluny Macpherson. In traditional Highland style, he welcomes them graciously.

Hungrily, they eat the venison[2] that Cluny offers. Then David sleeps while Cluny describes to Alan his life as an outlawed Jacobite rebel.

David stays in bed for days. He is weak, sick, and dizzy. Crossing Rannoch Moor has given him a dangerous fever.

While David rests, Alan and Cluny talk, play cards—and gamble enormous sums of money.

Alan loses all he has and asks to borrow David's last few coins. Out of friendship, David agrees, but he is very worried.

It was all daffing.[3]

Alan and Cluny play on, until Alan loses. Cluny says he'll give the money back—but this is deeply shameful for Alan.

The offer hurts Alan's pride and so causes Cluny to scorn him. David asks to talk to Cluny, alone.

It's a very painful thing to be placed in this position.

David explains that they desperately need the money Alan has lost to help them escape to France. At first Cluny is angry.

Here's my hand.

However, when he understands their plight, he praises David's courage in telling him.

1. Step in by: Please come in
2. venison: deer meat
3. all daffing: just a game

TWO FRIENDS QUARREL

> What are ye thinking?

Cluny's servant guides Alan and David through more wild, rugged mountains. Now they're heading south and east, toward the port of Queensferry.*

David is still feeling ill and is annoyed with Alan for gambling their money. Alan is ashamed that David had to speak to Cluny. They walk on, both sulking.

> Nothing!

> I'm no very keen to stay where I'm no wanted!

> It was you that was to blame.

David decides he wants to go his own way—Alan is too much trouble—but denies it when Alan asks.

Alan is really angry. He knows that David is lying, and David then feels guilty.

For weeks, the two friends have shared hardships and trusted each other. But now, they can't stop quarreling. Will tiredness and anger make them careless? One foolish move could betray them!

Cluny's servant leaves. Now they must find a path through the wilderness alone, in cold, wet, foggy weather—and keep away from Red Fox's soldiers!

They sleep all day and walk all night. It's extremely miserable. They shiver with cold, but they daren't light a fire in case the soldiers see it.

David still feels unwell. Alan offers to carry his bag, but David won't let him.

Defiantly, Alan starts to whistle a song about a famous Jacobite victory.

David says he doesn't care about Jacobites or their battles. Alan tells him to show more respect when talking to a man from a proud Jacobite family!

David loses his temper. He says that Jacobites—and all Highlanders—are dirty, smelly cowards. Alan can't ignore this insult! Furious, he draws his sword.

Ready?!

Come on!

Na, na—I cannae, I cannae.[1]

But Alan can't fight David. They are friends! And David's young and not trained in dueling.

Ohhh…

David drops his sword, too. He is too sick to go on quarreling.

Let me get my arm about ye.

David has difficulty breathing. He's got a pain in his side. He collapses, but Alan catches him. Alan had no idea that David was so ill. Now he fears that David may be dying.

Let's say no more about it!

Now I like ye better!

Shocked and horrified by their quarrel, they beg each other's forgiveness. Alan supports David as he totters down the hill, half laughing, half crying.

1. cannae: cannot

SAFE AT LAST

At last they reach a small, poor house, where Alan asks for shelter. The door is opened by a friendly clansman, Duncan Dhu Maclaren.

Duncan's wife puts David to bed and sends for a doctor. She cares for David until he feels better.

During the day, Alan hides in the woods—soldiers are still hunting him! But at night, he comes to Duncan's house to play the bagpipes with him.

Duncan and his wife keep Alan's visits a secret. But one night, a stranger comes.

It is Robin Oig, son of the famous outlaw, Rob Roy Macgregor. Rob Roy and Alan are old enemies!

You are a man of your sword?

When Alan arrives and sees Robin, they start insulting each other. Quickly, Duncan steps between them; he wants no fighting!

Robin Oig, ye are a great piper.

Robin and Alan are both keen bagpipe players, so Duncan suggests a musical challenge.

Cheerfully, they make music all night. Then, once again, it's time for Alan and David to leave.

They walk south for days, toward the city of Stirling.* There, they see the famous bridge over the River Forth.*

To reach Queensferry, they need to cross that bridge. But it is strongly guarded by English soldiers.

Dismayed, they leave Stirling and walk beside the river. They come to an inn, with a boat anchored close by.

They dare not trust the boatman; he might betray them to the soldiers. But at the inn they meet a bonnie lass selling bread and cheese.

She looks kind, so Alan asks her to help them. He pretends that David is ill and a hunted Jacobite rebel!

But David thinks it is better to tell her the truth. He explains he must cross the river to see a lawyer in Queensferry.

A very fine lass...

The girl has heard of the lawyer, so she decides to trust David. That night, she rows him and Alan safely across the river.

They've escaped! David is safe at last. But Alan looks rather regretful as the girl rows away.

Alan hides while David goes to look for the lawyer. They arrange to meet after dark, with a secret, whistled signal.

* See map on page 42

THE LAWYER'S STORY

It is quiet and peaceful in Queensferry, but David can't stop worrying. Is he really safe?

He goes to look for Rankeillor, the Balfour family lawyer. He sees a stout, sensible-looking man outside one of Queensferry's finest houses.

It is Rankeillor himself! He calls to David and walks over to question him. Who is he? Where does he come from?

David says he belongs to the Balfour family, of Shaws. He was kidnapped and his inheritance has been stolen.

Rankeillor has heard of David's disappearance. But is David's story true, or is he lying?

Rankeillor has heard different tales from Ebenezer and Hoseason. Ebenezer tells him that he has kindly sent David abroad to study.

But Hoseason swears that David drowned in a shipwreck off Mull.

Rankeillor asks David to tell him what has happened to him since he was kidnapped.

He is horrified to hear about David's adventures in the Highlands with Alan Breck, a dangerous Jacobite.

Even so, Rankeillor says he trusts David, and will look after him. He provides him with clean clothes, soap, and warm water.

After a wash, David changes out of the rags he's been wearing. He begins to feel like his old self again.

The matter hinges on a love affair…

Rankeillor is pleased. He sits David down and says he has an extraordinary story to tell him.

The Balfours were a fine family, rich and respected. They built a mansion, the house of Shaws, and owned farms and cottages.

They had two sons: Alexander, the firstborn, then Ebenezer. By law, Alexander was due to inherit the house of Shaws and its land because he was the eldest.

But Alexander and Ebenezer both fell in love with Grace, a pretty young lady. She preferred Alexander, who had a kind and gentle character.

Ebenezer was spoiled, jealous, mean, and selfish. He made such a fuss that Alexander offered to let him marry Grace instead.

Not surprisingly, Grace was angry. She told both brothers to leave her alone. She, not they, would choose who to marry!

Finally, they came to an agreement. Grace chose to marry Alexander without his inheritance; they were poor but happy. Ebenezer got the house and was rich—but miserable.

RIGHTFUL INHERITANCE

But, by law, Shaws should belong to David. Now David's father is dead, Ebenezer has no legal right to live there. How can they persuade him to go quickly and quietly?

David thinks he can do this, but only with help from Alan. They find him, and set off to the house of Shaws.

Alan knocks loudly on the front door, while the others hide nearby. Ebenezer refuses to talk until Alan mentions the name "David."

Alan says that his friends on the island of Mull* are keeping David prisoner. They'll free David, if Ebenezer pays them—or, if he prefers, they'll kill him!

Ebenezer says he doesn't want David killed because he's already given Captain Hoseason money to kidnap him.

The trick has worked! Ebenezer has confessed to a terrible crime. Rankeillor steps forward and congratulates Alan.

They tie Ebenezer to a chair and take away his gun. Now it is time to talk seriously.

Ebenezer has no choice. He will give David money now—and the house of Shaws after he dies.

Alan and David light a fire and find Ebenezer's wine cellar. They open some bottles to celebrate David's good fortune.

* See map on page 42
1. wasnae: was not

Now David has money, good friends, and a promising future. But what will happen to Alan? He is still in danger.

Rankeillor warns David: helping a Jacobite like Alan might get him hanged as a traitor. But David insists. He must help his friend.

Rankeillor suggests that they ask King George to pardon[1] Alan for being a Jacobite. He gives David a letter to take to a government lawyer in Edinburgh.

But Alan must stay in hiding for now. And, if David wants to help him, it must be done secretly.

David and Alan set off to walk by night from Queensferry to Edinburgh. This may be the last journey the friends make together.

At Edinburgh's city gates, they stop. It is too risky for Alan to enter the city until he gets a pardon.

Goodbye.

Well, goodbye.

Alan and David shake hands, slowly and thoughtfully. Then, one after the other, they turn and walk away. David daren't look back—if he does, he may cry.

Without Alan, David feels lost and alone. There's a cold chill around his heart. But he hopes, one day, to see his friend again—and to share more adventures!

The End

1. pardon: to forgive a crime

ROBERT LOUIS STEVENSON (1850–1894)

Robert Louis Stevenson was born in Edinburgh on November 13, 1850. He was the only son of Thomas Stevenson and his wife Margaret Isabella Balfour. Both families were wealthy, well educated, and deeply respectable. Robert's mother suffered from tuberculosis, and it is unclear whether she passed the disease on to him, or whether he suffered from another lung disorder. Either way, he was often too ill to attend school, and so lay in bed, reading or composing poems and stories of his own.

Robert Louis Stevenson, from an image held at Bishop Museum, Hawaii.

UNIVERSITY

Aged 17, he enrolled at Edinburgh University. His father wanted him to study engineering, but Robert wasn't eager; he wanted to be a writer. As a compromise, he studied law, but he spent all his spare time writing. During vacations he traveled to France to meet other young artists and writers. He was often ill but always active-minded, unconventional, and determined.

MARRIAGE

Robert qualified as a lawyer in 1875, but he never worked in the profession. His first book, about a canoeing expedition in France, was published in 1878, and he spent the rest of his life as a writer. In France, Robert also met the woman who would later become his wife: Fanny Van de Grift Osbourne, an American. They were a strange couple, but passionately in love. She was everything he was not: loud, healthy, and vibrant. Robert's family was not happy because Fanny was 11 years older than Robert and was already married. In 1880, after Fanny's divorce, Robert traveled to America to marry her. Robert's family was appalled, but the couple was happy together.

FIRST NOVEL

In 1881 Robert and Fanny traveled to Scotland with Fanny's son, Lloyd Osbourne. They made peace with Robert's family, and visited the Highlands with them. But the cold and rain worsened Robert's health, so they soon left in search of milder weather. They went to Switzerland, France, and the south of England, then back to America. All the time, Robert wrote—travel books, poems, and short stories.

Then, in 1883, he published his first long novel. Its title was *Treasure Island*. During the next six years, Robert wrote four more novels. These included his most famous work, *The Strange Case of Dr. Jekyll and Mr. Hyde*. A brilliant fantasy thriller, it was an instant bestseller and made him famous throughout Britain and the United States.

DETERIORATING HEALTH
By 1887, Robert's health was getting worse, so he and Fanny returned to America with his mother (his father had died). Then, with Fanny's children, they set sail across the Pacific Ocean.

SAMOA
After a long voyage, they settled on the island of Samoa. They built a house and made friends with the islanders, who called Robert "Tusitala" ("Teller of Tales"). Robert was fascinated by the islands, and their rich heritage of songs and stories. He collected information for a huge history of the Pacific, campaigned to stop Europeans ill-treating local people, and wrote poems and stories about the island. Robert also wrote novels set in faraway Scotland. The last of these, *Weir of Hermiston*, which he never finished, was probably his best piece of writing. Sadly, even the warm Pacific climate could not cure Robert's illness, and he died suddenly, on December 3, 1894—he was just 44 years old. He was buried on the top of Mount Vaea, above his home in Samoa, and lines from his own poem *Requiem* were carved on his tomb:

Under the wide and starry sky,
Dig the grave and let me lie.
Glad did I live and gladly die,
And I laid me down with a will.

Robert and Fanny Stevenson's tomb on the Pacific island of Samoa.

DAVID BALFOUR'S JOURNEY

*J*he Map below shows the journey taken by David Balfour around the Scottish coast and across the Highlands.

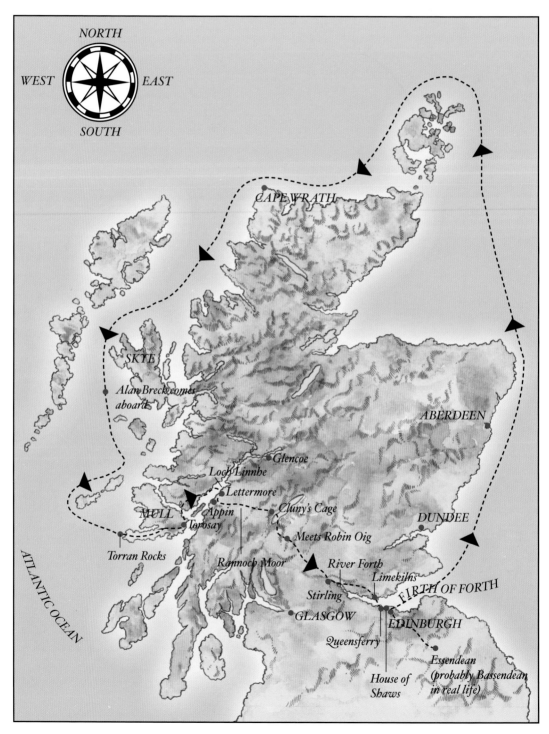

NORTH

WEST ✦ EAST

SOUTH

CAPE WRATH

SKYE

Alan Breck comes aboard

ABERDEEN

Glencoe

Loch Linnhe

Lettermore

MULL

Appin

Torosay

Cluny's Cage

DUNDEE

Meets Robin Oig

Torran Rocks

Rannoch Moor

River Forth

Limekilns

Stirling

FIRTH OF FORTH

ATLANTIC OCEAN

GLASGOW

EDINBURGH

Queensferry

Essendean (probably Bassendean in real life)

House of Shaws

The Jacobite Rebellions

*K*idnapped is set in the years soon after the Jacobite rebellion of 1745. This was the last in a series of uprisings led by princes descended from King James VII of Scotland (who was also James II of England). They claimed the right to be king. The name "Jacobite" comes from "Jacobus," the Latin form of "James." It means "supporter of James."

1685–1688
James VII/II rules Scotland, England, and Wales. He becomes a Roman Catholic; this is against the law. James is unpopular—even in Scotland—and does not rule well.

1689
James VII/II is exiled by Scottish and English politicians and replaced by his daughter Mary II and her husband, William of Orange; they are both Protestants.

1702
Mary II dies; James's second daughter, Anne (also a Protestant), becomes queen.

1707
The Act of Union, passed by both Scottish and English parliaments, joins Scotland to England and Wales, suspends the Scottish parliament, and sets up the United Kingdom of Great Britain.

1708
Jacobites led by Prince James Edward Stewart (son of James VII/II, and a Roman Catholic) try to invade by sea. They are defeated off the east coast of Scotland and escape to France.

1714
Queen Anne dies. United Kingdom parliament in London chooses George of Hanover (a German prince, close relative of Queen Anne, and a Protestant) to be King George I.

1715–1716
Prince James Edward Stewart, helped by the French, invades northeast Scotland; most Highlanders support him but are defeated at the Battle of Sheriffmuir, near Stirling.

1719
Jacobites, helped by Spain, invade northwest Scotland. They are defeated at the Battle of Glen Shiel, near Kyle of Lochalsh.

1745–1746
Jacobites led by Charles Edward Stewart, known as Bonnie Prince Charlie (son of Prince James Edward, grandson of James VII/II, and a Roman Catholic), land near Glenfinnan, in the far west of Scotland. Some Highlanders support them. They defeat George I's armies at the battles of Falkirk and Prestonpans (in central Scotland) but are slaughtered at the battle of Culloden, near Inverness. Prince Charlie hides in the Highlands, is helped to escape by Highland noblewoman Flora MacDonald, and never returns.

1748
United Kingdom parliament passes laws to ban old Highland traditions, weakening Highland chiefs' powers.

The Jacobite rebellions took place at a time when Scotland had just stopped being an independent nation and had been united with England and Wales. Lowland Scots welcomed this, and so did some Highlanders. They thought it would make Scotland richer and stronger. But the Jacobite princes realized that this would weaken their chances of ever becoming king.

The Jacobite rebellions were influenced by bitter religious quarrels. Most Scots and English were Protestants; they mistrusted Roman Catholics. But some Highlanders and some Jacobites were Catholics, like the Jacobite princes.

Most Jacobites, like Alan Breck, came from the Highland region. Life there was harsh and poor. Highlanders lived by fishing and farming and were fiercely loyal to their chiefs, the traditional leaders of their clans (large family groups sharing the same surname).

Life in Lowland Scotland, where David Balfour grew up, was very different. There were international ports, rich trading cities, and new manufacturing industries, as well as go-ahead farms. The Lowland city of Edinburgh, capital of Scotland, was a great center of science, law, medicine, education, and the arts. Lowlanders were proud of their lifestyle and thought that Highlanders were uncivilized. They supported King George I.

The Red Fox (Colin Campbell of Glenure)

Factor (estate manager) for the Duke of Argyll, chief of the Campbell clan. The Campbells were traditional enemies of the Jacobite Stewart clan and supported King George I. The Red Fox was on his way to evict some Campbell clan members from their homeland, as a punishment for being Jacobites, when he was murdered at Lettermore, near Ballachulish, on May 14, 1752.

Robin Oig Macgregor

Son of the famous outlaw Rob Roy (Red Rob) Macgregor (1671–1734). Like his father, Robin was a famous cattle thief and Jacobite supporter. But he was never so popular or well respected and was also accused of other, brutal crimes. He was hanged in Edinburgh in 1753.

Ewen "Cluny" MacPherson

Chief of the MacPherson clan. Out of loyalty, Cluny agreed to support Prince Charles Edward in 1745, but he did not think the Jacobite rebellion was wise. Cluny's home was burned down by King George's soldiers, so he built a hideout in wild mountain country. His clansmen helped him hide there for nine years. In 1755, Cluny finally escaped to France. He died there, very poor, in 1764.

James of the Glens (James Stewart of Aucharn)

Half-brother of the Stewart clan chief and a loyal Jacobite. Farmed land in Appin and was leader of the Stewart clansmen there. In 1752, James was (wrongly) accused of helping to murder the Red Fox and was hanged at Ballachulish. His body was left dangling from a tree, as a warning to passersby.

A view of the historic center of Edinburgh, with Edinburgh Castle in the background.

Timeline of World Events

During the Lifetime of Robert Louis Stevenson

1850
November 13—Robert Louis Balfour Stevenson born.
Thousands rush to California after gold is discovered there.

1851
Herman Melville writes his whaling adventure, *Moby-Dick*.

1853
Crimean War starts.

1858
India becomes part of the British Empire.
First telegraph (signals) cable laid under the Atlantic Ocean.

1859
Work begins on digging Suez Canal, which will link Mediterranean Sea to Red Sea and Indian Ocean.
Small states unite to create nation of Italy.
Charles Darwin writes his first book on evolution, *On the Origin of Species*.

1861
United States Civil War begins, between states for and against slavery.
Louis Pasteur discovers bacteria.

1865
U.S. Civil War ends; slavery banned.
President Abraham Lincoln assassinated.
Joseph Lister uses antiseptic to reduce infections after surgery.
Gregor Mendel makes pioneering study of genetics.

1866
Alfred Nobel invents dynamite.
United States purchases Alaska from Russia.

1867
Stevenson studies engineering at Edinburgh University.

1868
Revolution in Spain.

1871
Stevenson changes his studies from engineering to law.

1875
Stevenson qualifies as a lawyer.

1876
Alexander Graham Bell invents the telephone.

1878
Stevenson's first volume of work is published: *An Inland Voyage*, a piece of travel writing.

1879
Thomas Edison invents electric light.

1880
Stevenson marries Fanny Van de Grift Osbourne.

1881
Stevenson and Fanny go to Scotland.
"The Sea Cook" is published in *Young Folks*.

1883
Treasure Island is published as a book.

1886
The Strange Case of Dr. Jekyll and Mr. Hyde is published.
Kidnapped is published.

1887
George Eastman invents the Kodak camera.
Stevenson and Fanny return to the United States.

1889
Eiffel Tower built in Paris.
Stevenson and his family arrive and settle on Samoa, an island in the Pacific Ocean.
The Master of Ballantrae is published.

1894
December 3—Robert Louis Stevenson dies in Samoa, at age 44.

Robert Louis Stevenson also wrote a huge amount of poetry, essays, and travel writing, as well as the novels for which he is best known.

FILM VERSIONS OF *KIDNAPPED*

Kidnapped presents a romantic, simplified picture of the Jacobite uprisings and portrays Highlanders as wild, noble, brave, and loyal. Scotland's history is given similar treatment in the many films based on Stevenson's story.

1917
USA. Now lost, but said to leave out most of the story.

1929
USA. Cartoon version.

1938
USA. Said to be "a failure."

1948
USA. Said to be "striking and well-acted."

1949–1956
Six different versions made for television.

1960
USA/UK. Very faithful to the book. Starred Peter Finch as Alan Breck and Peter O'Toole as Robin Oig Macgregor.

1968
Germany. Renamed *Shots under the Gallows*.

1971
USA. Star-studded cast. Michael Caine controversial as Alan Breck. Mixed the story of *Kidnapped* with another of Stevenson's novels, *Catriona*.

1973
USA. Cartoon version.

1975
New Zealand. For television.

1978
Germany/France. Won great praise. Mixed the story of *Kidnapped* with *Catriona*.

1980
Scotland. For television.

1986
Australia. For television.

1995
USA. For television. Made many changes to original story.

2005
UK/New Zealand. For television. Mixed the story of *Kidnapped* with *Catriona*.

OTHER BOOKS WRITTEN BY R. L. STEVENSON

1878—*An Inland Voyage*
1879—*Travels with a Donkey in the Cévennes*
1883—*Treasure Island*
1884—*The Silverado Squatters*
1885—*A Child's Garden of Verses*
1885—*The Body Snatcher*
1886—*Kidnapped*

1886—*The Strange Case of Dr. Jekyll and Mr. Hyde*
1888—*The Black Arrow*
1889—*The Master of Ballantrae*
1892—*The Wrong Box*
1896—*Weir of Hermiston*
(published posthumously; Stevenson was working on this the day he died.)

Scene from the 1960 version of Kidnapped, *starring Peter Finch as Alan Breck.*

STEVENSON COPYRIGHT STAMPS

After Stevenson's death, his family inherited the copyright to his books. This meant that they were entitled to a small payment for each copy that was sold. To make sure that the money was collected, the Society of Authors printed these special stamps, which were stuck into copies of the books published between 1925 and 1944. Each stamp is printed with the amount of the copyright payment, in old pence.

Stamps of this kind are very common on old gramophone records, but are not usually found in books. Stevenson's stepson, Lloyd Osbourne, said that the system worked very well and he wished he had tried it sooner.

INDEX

FURTHER INFORMATION

IF YOU LIKED THIS BOOK, YOU MIGHT ALSO WANT TO TRY THESE
TITLES IN THE BARRON'S *GRAPHIC CLASSICS* SERIES:

Treasure Island
Oliver Twist
The Hunchback of Notre Dame
Moby Dick
Journey to the Center of the Earth

FOR MORE INFORMATION ON ROBERT LOUIS STEVENSON:

The National Library of Scotland
www.nls.uk

Stevenson House
www.stevenson-house.co.uk